PUFFIN BOOKS

Dustbin Charlie Cleans Up

Ann Pilling was brought up in industrial Lancashire, where many of her books are set, but has also lived in Wales, London, Buckinghamshire and on the east and west coasts of the USA. For some years she taught English, but has been writing since 1979. She now lives in Oxford with her husband, her two sons Ben and Thomas, their friend Vera and a budgerigar called Kit. She enjoys singing, cooking, listening to music, and gardening, especially when someone else does the weeding. Her favourite relaxation is walking in the Yorkshire Dales.

Dustbin Charlie Cleans Up

Ann Pilling

Illustrated by
Jean Baylis

PUFFIN BOOKS

PUFFIN BOOKS

Published by the Penguin Group
Penguin Books Ltd, 27 Wrights Lane, London W8 5TZ, England
Penguin Books USA Inc., 375 Hudson Street, New York, New York 10014, USA
Penguin Books Australia Ltd, Ringwood, Victoria, Australia
Penguin Books Canada Ltd, 10 Alcorn Avenue, Toronto, Ontario, Canada M4V 3B2
Penguin Books (NZ) Ltd, 182–190 Wairau Road, Auckland 10, New Zealand

Penguin Books Ltd, Registered Offices: Harmondsworth, Middlesex, England

First published by Viking 1994
Published in Puffin Books 1995
3 5 7 9 10 8 6 4 2

Filmset in Monophoto Times

Printed in England by Clays Ltd, St Ives plc

Contents

Messpot Grandad

Charlie was staying at
Grandad's house. He liked it.
Not much happened in the
country, where he lived on a
farm with his mum and dad.

But things were always
happening at Number 15
Union Street. That's where
Grandad lived, with Grandma.

Union Street was special. It was the place where Charlie could play with his favourite toy in the WHOLE WORLD!

Every day after breakfast, a shiny blue bus chugged past, full of shoppers. They were going to town and they always waved to Charlie. Then there was Curly Harry, the funny old tramp who did tricks in the park. He could juggle three

balls in the air at once *and* balance another on the end of his nose. Best of all was Frank the paper-boy, with his hair like black string. He took his papers round in an old pram. Charlie helped him once, and Frank paid him wages: three comics, all for himself.

Grandma was mad on cleaning. She said Grandad was a "messpot", and the day Charlie came to stay she was busy trying to smarten him up.

"You've got paint in your hair, Grandad," she fussed.

"And there's red rust all over your trousers. You're a *disgrace*!" And she flicked him clean with a big feather duster.

"Grandma," said Charlie, "can I go and play in the attic?" He wanted to say 'Hello" to his favourite toy.

But Grandma was a little bit
deaf. "You're right, dear," she
said, "I *am* getting rheumatic."
And she shook her duster out
of the window.

Grandad winked at Charlie. "She's spring-cleaning," he whispered. "Come on. Let's go down to my garage before she hoovers us up. You must meet Mildred. She's a beauty. You can play in the attic later on."

Mildred . . . Who could *that* be? Charlie felt rather worried as he followed Grandad down the garden path. Grandma wasn't called "Mildred" and she wasn't a "beauty" either. She was little and dumpy with a pink puffy face, soft white hair and eyes like currants, just like a sugar bun. She looked after Grandad beautifully though. He didn't like the sound of this Mildred at all.

Was she a dog? Or a cat? No. They didn't have any pets at Number 15 Union Street.

Grandma said dogs left hairs on everything, and cats made her sneeze.

He'd soon find out. Grandad was leading the way to the garage. "Here she is, here's Mildred," he said, pointing to a bulky white thing in the middle of the dusty floor. It was very big and very knobbly, and it was all covered up with an old sheet. It looked very mysterious *indeed*.

Charlie Meets Mildred

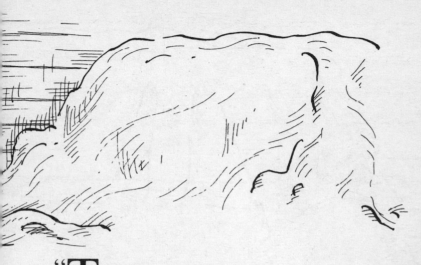

"Take a look," said
Grandad. "Go on, she won't
bite you."

Charlie crept forward,
feeling nervous. What if
Mildred jumped up at him? Or
went off pop? Grandad
sometimes played tricks.

27

Gingerly Charlie lifted one
corner of the sheet. He could
see a rusty headlamp. Then he
lifted a bit more sheet. This
time he uncovered an old brass
horn with a rubber thing on the
end. He could smell leather
now, and polish.

Grandad was getting a bit impatient. "Come on, Mildred," he said, "let's have a proper look at you." He suddenly whisked off the sheet and threw it in a corner.

"Wow!" whispered Charlie. Mildred wasn't a giant dog or a monster cat. And she wasn't an elephant and she wasn't a dinosaur either. She was the most fabulous old car he had ever seen! She was very dirty though. Grandma wouldn't approve at all.

"Go on, sit behind the

wheel," said Grandad.

So Charlie climbed in and
got comfy in the squishy
leather seat. Then he pressed
the rubber bulb thing.

32

"Poop, poop," murmured Mildred dreamily.

"Does she go, Grandad?" he said. He was excited now. He wanted Mildred to take them for a spin.

"Oh *yes*," Grandad told him. "But she needs cleaning up. I've got to polish the seats. They're real leather. Then there's the outside too. When she's ready, I'm going to enter her for the Old Car Race. You can help me. Here, have a duster."

So Charlie got busy,
polishing the big brass
headlamps. It was fun,
cleaning Mildred. But inside he
felt muddled. Quite a big bit of

him wanted to climb up to the
attic, to see if his special friend,
his favourite toy in the
WHOLE WORLD, was still
there.

"Grandad," he said, when
the headlamp was all shiny
again, "can I go and have a
little peep in the attic now?"

"All right, Sunshine," said
Grandad, and he puffed up the
stairs after him. "Sunshine"
meant Grandad was in a good
mood. It was because of
Mildred.

The attic was all cobwebby.

Grandma hadn't reached it yet
with her feather duster. In a
corner, sitting on a box, was
Tin Man, the wonderful
walking toy who had once
gone all the way down Union
Street by himself.

"Hello, Tin Man,"
whispered Charlie, and he gave
the toy a little prod. He was so
pleased to see Tin Man again
he couldn't believe he was real.

"You're awfully *dusty*," he added. Then he looked round for something to rub the dirt away.

But Grandad was checking his watch. "Come on, Charlie," he said. "We've got to get Mildred cleaned up." He didn't seem very interested in poor Tin Man.

Soon they were back at the garage and Grandad was making big clashy noises with the up-and-over doors.

"Jump in," he shouted. "We're off to the carwash. Mildred's got to be extra specially clean for the Old Car Race."

Charlie Gets a Shock

WALTER'S WONDER CARWASH

MAX. HEAD ROOM

WALTERS
WONDER
CARWASH
SUPA . 2.00
SUPA 3.00
SUPA DUPA 5.00

So Charlie jumped in, and off
they went. Mildred made a
funny rattly sound as they
drove along, and Grandad
frowned. But it was lovely,
bouncing up and down on the

big puffy seats. They smelt like
new shoes. People on the road
stared as they drove past.
Some waved. It's like being the
Queen, thought Charlie.

"Is the carwash just a big
water-pipe?" he said as they
rattled along. Their car didn't
get cleaned much, out in the
country. Sometimes Dad

swooshed water over it with the
rubber hose he used to fill the
cows' trough, and sometimes
Mum did it with a sponge and
bucket.

"Oh no," said Grandad.
"They have great big brushes.
You just drive in and sit there."

"*And get washed?*"

"That's right. It's all electric.
You'll love it. Here we are."

Grandad turned Mildred in
at the gates of Walter's
Wonder Carwash.

"Drive straight in," shouted
Walter, taking Grandad's

money. "I'll give you a Wash, Dry 'n' Polish, cheapest in town."

Carefully, Grandad steered

Mildred's wheels on to some big rollers. Then he shut all the windows. Someone came and cleaned the mud off the glass

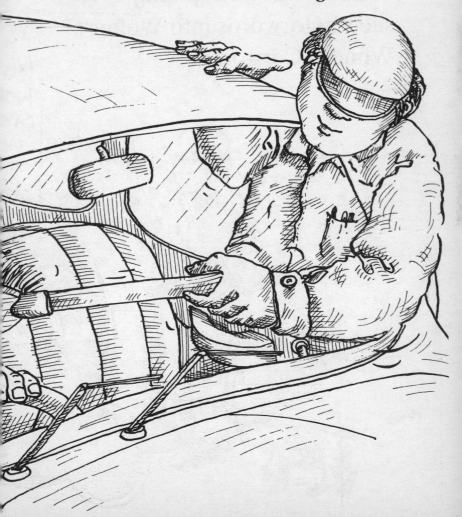

with a scrubbing-brush on a
long handle, pressed some
buttons and they were off.
Mildred was now gliding
silently forwards into Walter's
Wonder Carwash.

It was fun at first. On each
side there were pipes full of
holes, and out of the holes
came water in little jets. You
could see it all swishing over

the car, but you were safe and
dry inside. Soon Mildred was
very wet indeed.

"Now for the brushes," said
Grandad.

At first they were just green
soggy things on long stalks, but
suddenly they all reared up,
grew much bigger and bushier,
and started to twirl round and
round. They looked like great
big Christmas trees and they
were coming straight for
Charlie.

"Stop!" he shouted. "I don't
like this, Grandad." Mildred
was old, her glass might break
and then the terrible Christmas
trees would come in and get
him.

But she just glided on.

Grandad patted his hand.
"Don't worry," he said. "All
that dust has to be got off
before the Old Car Race.
They're only brushes, Charlie.
Look, they've finished now."
And, like magic, the Christmas
trees went away, turning back
into soggy stalk things. Then a
gentle whirring noise began.
Mildred was being dried and
polished.

She looked beautiful when
they drove away. Grandma
came out into Union Street to
admire her. "This is the

cleanest car I've ever seen," she said.

It was bangers and chips for tea, Charlie's favourite, but he could hardly eat any. When he thought about those enormous Christmas trees coming to get him he felt all wobbly inside.

And he dreamed about them
that night. Mildred didn't like
them either, so he drove her
away from Walter's Wonder

Carwash to their farm, where he cleaned the mud off very gently with Mum's yellow sponge. In the dream, Tin Man helped him. He did miss him, stuck up there in the attic, all alone. He wanted to *play* with him.

Treasure in
the Attic

Next day he got his chance.
Grandad was busy with
Mildred's insides. He was
trying to get rid of that rattly
noise. Charlie couldn't help – it
was all to do with oil and

screws. At last he was allowed
to go up to the attic by himself.
Grandma wanted some boxes.
She was collecting jumble for
people.

"Don't get dirty, Charlie!"
she shouted as he climbed the
stairs. She was still mad on
cleaning.

Charlie didn't bother about boring old cardboard boxes. He went straight over to Tin Man and put his arms round him. Tin Man was special.

He'd found him in a skip last
time he'd come to Grandad's.
But there'd been no room for
him to go back to the farm in
Grandad's little car. He'd had
to be left behind.

Charlie wound up the key in his back and he made a whirring noise. *His* insides were all right, but he really was very rusty and dirty again, after sitting in the attic for so long.

Charlie scrunched up some
newspaper and tried to get him
clean. But it was no good.
What he needed was a really
good scrub.

At tea-time he asked Grandad about it. "Have you got any special stuff to clean Tin Man? He's all rusty."

"Hmm," said Grandad. "Rust needs brushes, and the best brushes round here are at Walter's Wonder Carwash."

"Not those *Christmas* trees," said Charlie. He didn't really want to go to Walter's again. The huge green brushes had given him bad dreams.

But Grandad had an idea. "Mildred's engine's working nicely now," he said, "but she's

got all dirty again, after standing in my garage. I can't enter her in the Old Car Race without giving her another clean-up, can I? I think she

ought to have Walter's Supa
Dupa Wash this time, the one
that costs five pounds."

"But what about Tin Man?"
asked Charlie.

"Tin can?" said Grandma.

"Tin *Man*," repeated
Charlie. "He's all dirty."

"I know. That's why he lives
in the attic. I can't have rusty
marks on my furniture,
Charlie."

"But I want him to stay in my bedroom with me, like he used to," Charlie whispered, and a little tear rolled down his cheek. Mildred was fun, but she wasn't the same as Tin Man. And now Grandma was saying he was too dirty to live in the house.

"What about Tin Man?" he said again, pulling at Grandad's sleeve.

"Oh, didn't I tell you? He can come too. He can sit on top."

"Really?" said Charlie. He couldn't believe it.

"*Really*," answered Grandad with a wink.

So they got busy straight away. With a few rusty creaks and groans Tin Man walked into the garage all by himself, then Charlie helped Grandad lift him up on to Mildred's roof.

She had a special holder there,
for bicycles and trunks, but this
time it was Tin Man who was
strapped into place.

Off they went to the
carwash, with Tin Man sitting
proudly on top. Everyone
stared at them as they drove

along. People had seen old cars like Mildred before, but they'd never seen one with a Tin Man sitting on the roof!

At Walter's Wonder Carwash she got *two* washes. First the pipes sent water hissing all over her, then the Christmas trees

started. Their green branches
spread out stiffly and they
whizzed round and round as
they came nearer and nearer.

"Are you all right, Tin
Man?" shouted Charlie.
"Don't fall off!" Now he knew
they were only brushes he
didn't mind so much. And
something had to get that little
old Tin Man clean again.

Mildred looked beautiful
after her wash. So did Tin
Man. Walter's Supa Dupa
Special was value for money.

And when it was time for

WALTER'S WONDER CARWASH

Charlie to go back to the farm
he got a big surprise. Tin Man
wasn't sent back to the attic.
He came home with them.

Grandma came too, and she
brought so many suitcases that
they had to put Tin Man on top
again. It was a very long drive
but, do you know, he didn't fall
off *once*!

DUSTBIN CHARLIE

Ann Pilling

"Is a skip bigger than a dustbin?"
"*Much* bigger."
"Well, they're getting one for
Number 10."

Charlie had always liked seeing what
people threw out in their dustbins. So
he's thrilled to find the toy of his dreams
among the rubbish in the skip. But
during the night, someone else takes it.

Also in Young Puffin

CUP FINAL FOR CHARLIE

Joy Allen

Two adventures for Charlie – both with surprising endings!

Uncle Tim turns up with a spare ticket for the Cup Final at Wembley. But will Charlie be allowed to go?

Then Charlie is given a brand-new pair of shiny red boots, which turn out to be far more useful than anyone could have imagined!

Also in Young Puffin

The ELM STREET Lot

Philippa Pearce

"Off to mischief, I suppose?"

Mr Crackenthorpe was a surly old fellow, but he might have been forgiven for his suspicions. For the Elm Street gang were always in on the action, whether they were tracking down a lost hamster, being galley-slaves in a brand-new bathtub, or going on safari across the roof-tops!

Also in Young Puffin

MICHAEL
and the Jumble-Sale Cat

Marjorie Newman

A new mum and dad for Michael!

Michael lives in the children's home with
his best friend Lee and his precious
jumble-sale cat. One day Jenny, his social
worker, asks him if he'd like to live with
a new family and Michael is thrown into
confusion. But when the day arrives for
him to leave the children's home, he is
both sad and glad. His new family turn
out to be very special indeed!